OYCE DUNBAR has written over seventy books for children including the *Mouse and Mole* books, which were adapted into a television series. She lives in Norwich.

BARTON has illustrated many bestselling books for children including the ard-winning *In The Rain With Baby Duck*. She lives and works in Devon.

D0184141
1804131102

To my dear friend, Magdalen Russell – J.D.

For Natalie and Jonny and the two bad cats, Andre and Leo – J.B.

Text copyright © Joyce Dunbar 2012
Illustrations copyright © Jill Barton 2012
The right of Joyce Dunbar to be identified as the author and of Jill Barton
to be identified as the illustrator of this work has been asserted by them in accordance
with the Copyright, Designs and Patents Act, 1988 (United Kingdom).

First published in Great Britain in 2012 and in the USA in 2013 by
Frances Lincoln Children's Books,
74–77 White Lion Street, London, N1 9PF
www.franceslincoln.com

This paperback edition first published in the UK in 2013

All rights reserved

No part of this publication may be reproduced, stored in a retrieval system, or transmitted,
in any form, or by any means, electrical, mechanical, photocopying, recording or otherwise
without the prior written permission of the publisher or a licence permitting restricted copying.
In the United Kingdom such licences are issued by the Copyright Licensing Agency,
Saffron House, 6–10 Kirby Street, London EC1N 8TS.

A catalogue record for this book is available from the British Library.

ISBN 978-1-84780-492-1

Illustrated with pencil and watercolour

Set in Latina MT

Printed in China

1 3 5 7 9 8 6 4 2

Puss Jekyll Cat Hyde

Joyce Dunbar

Illustrated by Jill Barton

FRANCES LINCOLN
CHILDREN'S BOOKS

This is Puss Jekyll

Pet of the house.

Hear her purr

As she grooms

Her fur,

Or curls

On my lap

For a nap.

Furry, purry puss.

So tame, I think

She is almost

One of

Us.

Now comes Cat Hyde

Scourge of the mouse.

Hear her howl

On her midnight

Prowl.

See her crouch

Then pounce

All fang and claw,

See the poor little

House mouse

Dangling

From her

Jaw.

This is Puss Jekyll

Dozy, lazy

Snoozy puss.

So cosy.

Any warm spot

In the house

Will do.

The plump cushion

Or wicker chair

Or that sunny

Dappled

Patch

On the stair.

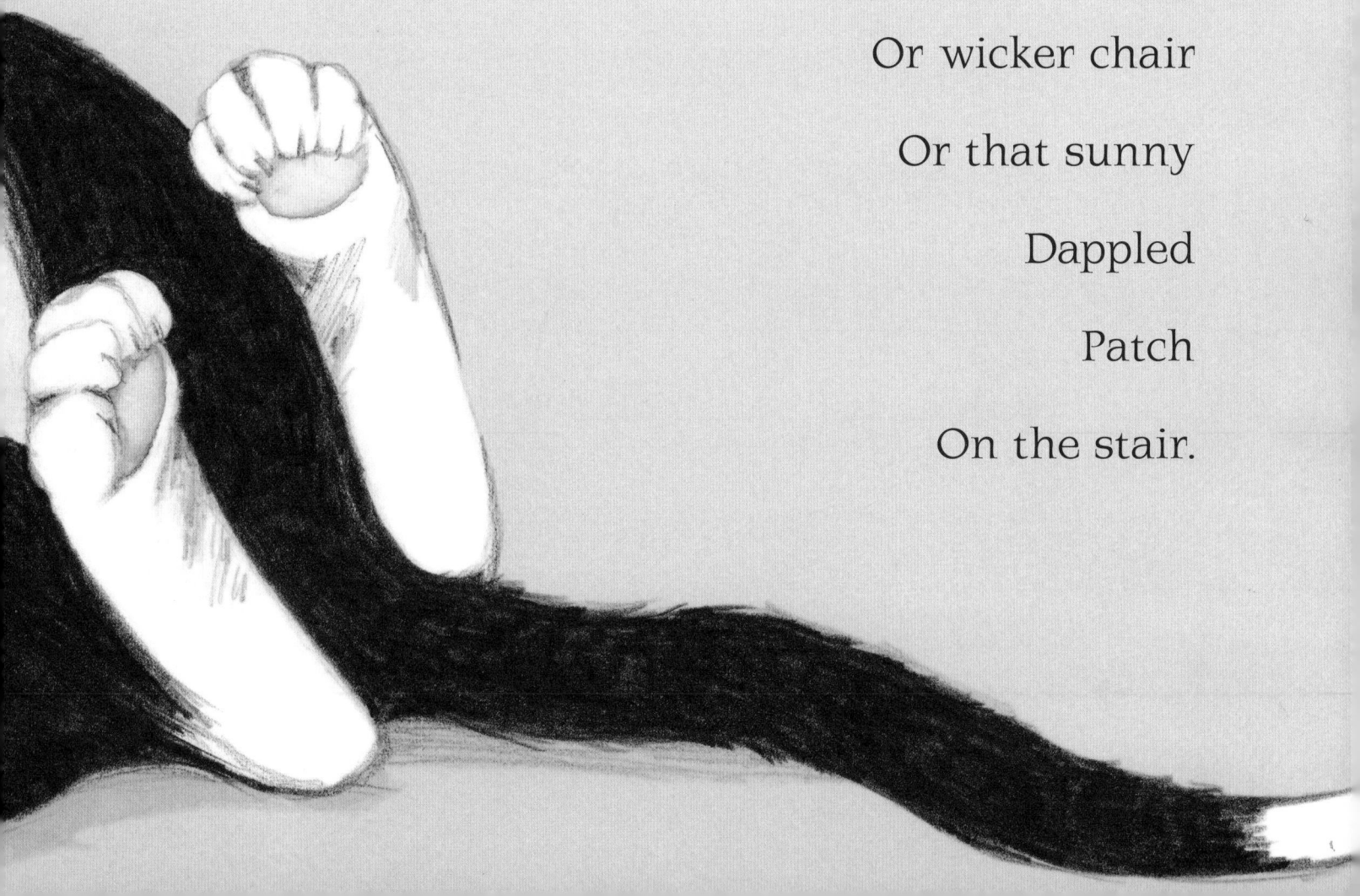

Now comes Cat Hyde

Ears pricked

Eyes wide.

Piercing

The dark

So stark

Scaring

Daring.

Oh she can outglare

The barefaced moon

The owl

Or the fox

In his lair.

This is Puss Jekyll.

See the pink

Of a little tongue-tip

Lapping up

Sippy-sip, milk

From a bowl.

Then a wide

Wipe of nose

And whiskers

Face so clean

So saintly

Quaintly

Serene.

Now woe betide

Here comes Cat Hyde.

Pad pad

Through the mud

On the scent

On the track

Of blood

Fear and bone

Hunting the lone

Vole or shrew.

Anything tiny

And trembling

Will do.

This is Puss Jekyll

So charming

Disarming

Chasing

Skitter-scatter

That ball of wool

On the rug.

Then with a

Nonchalant

Innocent

Shrug

Folds in her claws

Tucks in her paws

So snug.

Now comes Cat Hyde

A warning in her

Sharp-toothed yawning.

Ravager

Savager

Devil cat, fiend

Sly

Schemer and spoiler

Of dreams.

Not for her the quick

Clean kill

But a long, lingering

Merciless thrill.

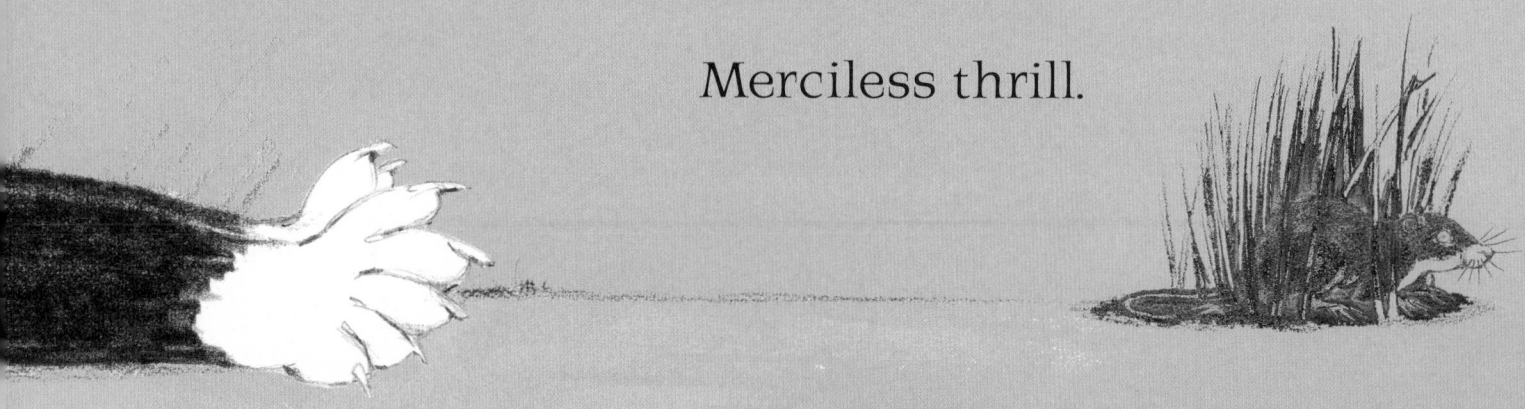

This is Puss Jekyll

So refined,

With such grace,

She puts never a paw

Out of place.

How she soothes,

Bewitches,

Beguiles,

With her smooth,

Velvety wiles.

Sleek, sweet

Pussikins,

So meek and mild.

This is Cat Hyde

Night stalker

Roof walker

Fearless

Tearless

Street fighter

War torn

Love worn

Battered and

Tattered

Adored passionara

So wicked

And wild.

This is Puss Jekyll

Nuzzles up

Nose to nose.

How we love

To be close

Me and my pet!

And yet . . .

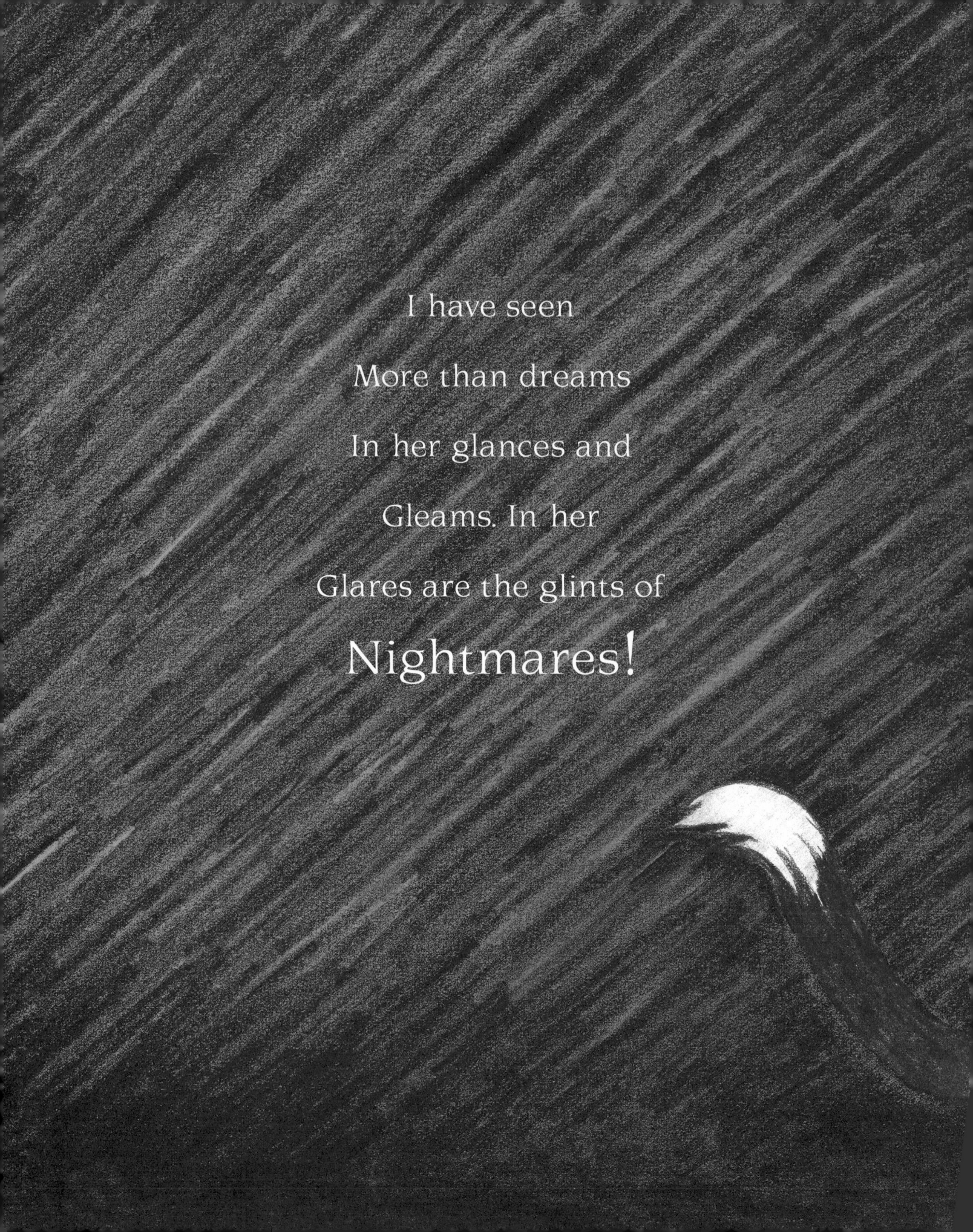

I have seen

More than dreams

In her glances and

Gleams. In her

Glares are the glints of

Nightmares!

Puss Jekyll, Cat Hyde

One cat, two names

One wild, one tame.

Come the night

She changes faces

Casting off

Her daytime graces.

Who is to blame

That my dear little

Kittikins

And this lynx-like

Minx-like

Sphynx-like

Deceiver . . .

Are one
and the
same?